This Little Tiger
book belongs to:

_____

_____

For Mark and Annemarie,
who love elephants (and cheese)! – T W

LITTLE TIGER PRESS LTD
an imprint of the Little Tiger Group
1 Coda Studios
189 Munster Road, London SW6 6AW
www.littletiger.co.uk

First published in Great Britain 2015
This edition published 2018
Text and illustrations copyright © Tim Warnes 2015
Visit Tim Warnes at www.ChapmanandWarnes.com
Tim Warnes has asserted his right to be identified
as the author and illustrator of this work under
the Copyright, Designs and Patents Act, 1988
A CIP catalogue record for this book is
available from the British Library
All rights reserved

ISBN 978-1-84869-053-0
LTP/1800/2260/0218
Printed in China
10 9 8 7 6 5 4 3

Disguises

The Great Cheese Robbery

Tim Warnes

LITTLE TIGER
LONDON

Daddy Elephant was as big
and strong as a tractor.
Patrick was small and only
a little bit strong.
Patrick was scared of lots
of things, like the dark,
ghosties, bees, and the fluff
you find under the sofa.

Daddy wasn't scared of anything.

Patrick tried and tried to make Daddy Elephant jump, but it never worked.

"It's not fair," sighed Patrick.
"You're not scared of anything!"

But there was **ONE** thing that scared
Daddy Elephant . . .

One afternoon there was a squeak at the door.

"Look, Daddy," gasped Patrick. "A teeny-tiny elephant!"

"That's not an elephant," cried Daddy.

IT'S A M-M-M-MOUSE!

"Good day, gentlemen," said the mouse. "My name is Cornelius J. Parker, from the Cheese Inspection Council. I'm here to inspect your cheese."

"W-w-we haven't got any," stammered Daddy Elephant.

"Yes we have," said Patrick helpfully, "in the fridge. I'll show you."

Cornelius J. Parker made a very thorough inspection indeed.

Cornelius opened his briefcase and pulled out a walkie-talkie.

Soon there was another
squeak at the door.

"We're 'ere for the fridge,"
said a stocky mouse.

"The fridge?" asked Patrick.

"We're confiscating it on
grounds of health and
safety," said the skinny one.

"B-b-but I'm making macaroni cheese tonight," said Daddy.

"It's his signature dish," Patrick added.

"Not any more, it's not!" said Cornelius.

Mascarpone! Manchego! Follow me!

"Don't worry – I'll help!"
called Patrick.

Suddenly there was a loud cry from the lounge.

The mice had a dastardly plan.

and not just the fridge. The mice took the telly, the phone, the fish, the biscuits, the lamp . . .

even Patrick's toys!

But they're MINE!

Sorry, kid. Boss said to take the lot!

Daddy Elephant gave a little whimper as the mice cheered and lifted up the sofa.

Patrick shouted in his biggest, strongest voice.
But the mice took no notice.

Just at that moment . . .

... Mummy Elephant appeared.

"Put my husband down OR ELSE!"
shouted Mummy Elephant.

Everybody froze.

Cornelius narrowed his eyes.
"Or else, what?"

Patrick's Mummy took a big,
deep breath and . . .

"The truth is, Patrick," said Mummy Elephant, "everyone's afraid of something – even your big old dad!"

"But he's still the biggest, strongest elephant around," said Patrick.

"I am," smiled Daddy proudly. "But when it comes to mice . . .

Mummy's the bravest!"